Clifford THE BIG RED DOG®

Clifford®
Finds a Clue

Clifford®
Finds a Clue

Adapted by Gail Herman from the television script
"To Catch a Bird" by Meg McLaughlin
Illustrated by Steve Haefele

**Based on the Scholastic book series
"Clifford The Big Red Dog"
by Norman Bridwell**

SCHOLASTIC INC.

New York   Toronto   London   Auckland   Sydney
Mexico City   New Delhi   Hong Kong   Buenos Aires

Copyright © 2004 Scholastic Entertainment Inc.
All rights reserved. Based on the CLIFFORD THE BIG RED DOG book series
published by Scholastic Inc. ™ and © Norman Bridwell.
SCHOLASTIC and associated logos are trademarks
and/or registered trademarks of Scholastic Inc.
CLIFFORD, CLIFFORD THE BIG RED DOG, and associated logos are trademarks
and/or registered trademarks of Norman Bridwell.

ISBN 0-439-53045-8

10 9 8 7 6 5 4   04 05 06 07 08 09

Designed by Peter Koblish
Printed in the U S A
First printing, March 2004

Contents

And the Winner Is . . .

The sun was high in the sky. Emily Elizabeth squinted. The school yard was so bright! She could hardly see the children sitting in front of her.

Emily Elizabeth and her friend Jetta stood on a small stage. They were the last two contestants in the Birdwell Island spelling contest.

"I'm proud of how well everyone has done today," said their teacher, Miss Carrington.

"And now only Emily Elizabeth and Jetta are left."

Miss Carrington smiled at the girls. "Okay, Emily Elizabeth," she continued. "Spell the word *monkey*."

Emily Elizabeth took a deep breath. "Monkey," she said. "M-O-N-K-E-E. Monkey."

"Oooh." Miss Carrington shook her head sadly. "I'm sorry, Emily Elizabeth. That's incorrect." She turned to Jetta. "Jetta? Spell the word *monkey*."

"Monkey," repeated Jetta. "M-O-N-K-E-Y. Monkey."

"Correct!" Miss Carrington said.

"Yessss!" Jetta pumped her fist in the air, excited.

The crowd clapped and cheered.

"Congratulations, Jetta," said Miss Carrington. She placed a gold medal around Jetta's neck. The medal gleamed in the sunshine. "You're the winner of our spelling contest!"

"Great job, Jetta," Emily Elizabeth said, shaking her friend's hand. She gazed at the medal. "Your medal sure is beautiful."

Jetta tossed her ponytail over her shoulder. The medal bounced, catching more sunlight. "I know."

Squawk! A seabird, perched on the school roof, stared at the shiny medal. Jetta grinned even wider. *Everybody* was admiring her beautiful new medal.

🦴 School's Out!

Three o'clock. The school bell rang. Children grabbed their backpacks and raced outside. Some kids headed home or to a friend's house. Some went to play in the park.

Emily Elizabeth and Jetta left the school together. A few minutes later, they passed the park.

"Hey, guys!" Their friend

Charley ran over, holding a soccer ball.

"Hi, Charley," said Emily Elizabeth.

Jetta rubbed her medal so it glowed even brighter. "Hello."

Charley bounced the soccer ball on his knee. "Want to play?" he asked.

"Sounds fun," said Emily Elizabeth. "But Mom and I are going shopping this afternoon."

"I'll play!" Jetta told Charley.

"But I'd better take off my championship spelling medal first."

Jetta carefully placed her medal in her sweater pocket. Then she turned to Emily Elizabeth.

"Would you please put this on the bench for me?" she asked in a sweet voice. "I don't want to lose my beautiful, shiny medal while I'm playing soccer."

Emily Elizabeth held out her arms and took the sweater.

"Come on!" Charley shouted. "Let's go!"

He and Jetta ran off, while Emily

Elizabeth carried the sweater to the bench. She set it down carefully.

Squawk!

The seabird cried out again.

Emily Elizabeth turned to leave. She didn't notice that the medal was poking out of Jetta's pocket, sparkling and shiny.

🦴 Something's Wrong

Later that afternoon, Jetta came home from the park.

"Woof!" Mac jumped up to say hello. He sniffed Jetta's sweater pocket.

"No, Mac." Jetta laughed. "There are no Tummy Yummies in there. Just my shiny new medal. I'll show you."

Jetta reached into her pocket. She felt around. Then she gasped. "My medal! It's gone!"

She turned the pocket inside out. But the medal was really and truly gone.

"And I bet I know who took it," Jetta said grimly.

Meanwhile, Clifford The Big Red Dog chewed on a giant bone. Emily Elizabeth had brought it home for him.

T-Bone was visiting Clifford. And little T-Bone was working

hard to get a piece of the Clifford-
sized treat.

"This bone is great!" said T-Bone.

"Yeah!" Clifford agreed. "I wish
Cleo was here to help us chew
it up."

"Hi, guys!" Cleo suddenly said,
walking into the backyard.

Surprised, T-Bone stopped chewing. "Wow, Clifford. Neat trick!"

"Sorry I'm late," Cleo explained. "I was at the pet groomer's."

Clifford sniffed. Cleo's poodle fur smelled clean and fresh. And she wore a brand-new bow.

Clifford squinted. Brightly colored stones decorated Cleo's bow. They glinted in the sunlight, making sparkling patterns on the ground.

"Wow!" T-Bone shaded his eyes

with his paw. "Your new bow sure
is shiny, Cleo!"

"You could send a secret
message with that bow!" Clifford
told Cleo.

"A secret message?" T-Bone
repeated.

"With a bow?" said Cleo.

Clifford sat up straight, excited.
"Yeah! Like in the book Emily

Elizabeth just read to me! These two children were being detectives, and one had a shiny bow like Cleo's. They were out looking for clues . . . when they realized they were late for lunch. So they used the bow to signal for help. They held it so it sparkled in a special pattern, to send a secret message."

Clifford smiled. "You could do the same thing, Cleo."

Cleo bounced on her paws. "I'd love to be a detective! Wouldn't you, T-Bone?"

T-Bone didn't answer for a minute. "I don't know," he said slowly. "Would I have to wear a shiny bow?"

Clifford laughed. Then he gazed over his friends' heads. "Look. Here come Jetta and Mac."

The two were marching up to Emily Elizabeth's front door.

"Jetta looks kind of mad," Clifford said. He took a closer look. Mac did, too. What was going on?

🦴 A Missing Medal

Mac looked at Clifford. Quickly, he strode over.

"Hey, Mac," Clifford said. "What's going on?"

"Oh, not much," Mac said. "Emily Elizabeth just stole Jetta's spelling medal."

"What?" Clifford was shocked.

"She took it from Jetta's sweater pocket at the park."

Clifford shook his head hard. His giant ears swung back and

forth. "Emily
Elizabeth would
never take her
medal."

A moment later,
Emily Elizabeth answered the
door. She listened to Jetta. Then
she shook her head, too.

"I would never take your
medal."

Jetta narrowed her eyes.
"You were jealous because
I won the spelling contest.
So you stole it!"

Emily Elizabeth tried to stay

calm. "I did not. Maybe you dropped it on the way home."

Jetta wrinkled her nose, confused. "Are you sure you didn't take it?"

Emily Elizabeth held up her hand to show she was telling the truth. "I promise."

Jetta's shoulders slumped. "I just can't believe it's gone."

"Well, I could help you

look for it," Emily Elizabeth offered.

Jetta shrugged. "Okay. Come on, Mac!" she called. "We're going to find my medal."

Even though we already know who has it, Mac thought. Without looking back, he followed Jetta and Emily Elizabeth down the street.

Clifford gazed after him, astonished. "Mac really thinks Emily Elizabeth stole that medal!"

Sniffing for Clues

Clifford was upset. He hung his head, casting a shadow over the entire house.

"Don't worry about Mac," T-Bone told him. "We know Emily Elizabeth didn't take it."

"I'm sure they'll find it," Cleo added.

All at once, Clifford brightened. "Wait! What if *we* found it?!"

T-Bone blinked. "How could we do that?"

"We could be detectives! Like in that book!"

Cleo wagged her tail. "Oh, detectives! I love it!"

"We'll start by looking around the park." Clifford took off. He ran so fast, the ground shook.

"Wait!" called Cleo and T-Bone. "Wait for us!"

At the park, Clifford put his giant nose to the ground. *Sniff! Sniff!* He was trying to find the scent left by Jetta's medal.

SNIFF!

The force pulled at Cleo's and T-Bone's fur like a vacuum cleaner. They struggled to stay in place.

Then they sniffed, too.

"This was the last place Jetta saw the medal," Clifford said. "Do you smell anything?"

T-Bone gave another sniff. "Like what?"

"Like clues, T-Bone!" Cleo answered.

"What's a clue?"

Cleo sighed. "Anything that will help lead us to Jetta's medal."

"Oh," said T-Bone, still not sure. But he kept sniffing.

A moment later, T-Bone stopped by the bench. A feather lay on the ground next to it.

Hmmm, thought T-Bone. He sniffed really hard, trying to figure things out. *Whoosh!* The feather sailed up his nose.

Aaaah-choo! T-Bone sneezed.

The feather flew back out. T-Bone watched it float to the ground.

"Is this a clue?" he asked.

Clifford eyed the feather. "Maybe . . ."

Meanwhile, Cleo was busy sniffing, too. "Hey!" she called from the other side of the bench.

"There's a really strong scent here!"

Clifford forgot the feather. He ran to Cleo. *Sniff!*

The scent was so strong! "Whoa!" he cried.

"This must be the last place Jetta saw her medal!" exclaimed Cleo.

"Come on!" said Clifford. "Let's follow that smell!"

On the Trail

The dogs walked in a line, sniffing the ground. Clifford went first, then Cleo, then T-Bone. When they came to the street, they stopped. They looked one way, then the other. And then they continued.

Soon they came to the center of town. T-Bone sniffed in front of the movie theater. He grinned.

Yum! Something tasty was over here!

Nose to the ground, T-Bone followed a trail of popcorn. He snapped up each piece of popcorn in his way. But T-Bone was going one way, and Clifford and Cleo were going the other way.

Cleo ran over and nudged T-Bone back into line.

Clifford padded past some shops. He was determined to find the medal. So determined, he didn't notice a lamppost in his way. He kept going, squeezing himself between the post and the building.

"Ooh!" he said, finally realizing he was stuck.

"Ooph!" said Cleo, bumping into Clifford.

"Ugh!" said T-Bone, bumping into Cleo.

"Ooh!" Clifford said again, pushing himself through.

Quickly, he put his nose back to the ground. He sniffed and sniffed, as Cleo and T-Bone followed close behind.

The scent was getting stronger

now. The dogs walked a few more blocks. At last, they reached the ferry dock.

Cleo took the lead. "The smell is getting stinkier!" she called to her friends.

"Cleo sure is a good sniffer!" T-Bone said.

"Ruuuuf!" Cleo barked excitedly.

Clifford grinned. "I think she found Jetta's medal!"

T-Bone shook his head, pointing a paw at the dock. "That's not Jetta's medal. That's Jetta."

Cleo was sniffing the ground under a bench — right by Jetta's feet!

"Stop sniffing me!" Jetta told Cleo. "And go away!"

Cleo made a face and doubled back to Clifford and T-Bone. "Well, there's no medal over there."

Clifford sat down. He was thinking about what to do next. What would a real detective do? One thing was sure. He wasn't going to give up.

"Come on," he told his friends. "Let's go back to my house. We need a new plan!"

🦴 Another Missing Object

Jetta and Emily Elizabeth sat quietly by the dock. Jetta sighed. She took out a shiny silver mirror and stared at her reflection. The mirror glinted in the sun.

"I'm sorry we didn't find your medal," Emily Elizabeth told her.

Jetta sighed even louder. "My neck is so bare without it," she complained. She looked once more in the mirror. Then she set it on the bench.

"Are you absolutely sure you didn't take it, Emily Elizabeth?"

Emily Elizabeth shook her head. "I said I didn't. And it really hurts my feelings when you keep asking."

Emily Elizabeth had to raise her voice to be heard. A seabird was squawking loudly right above their heads. A feather floated past the girls, settling on the ground.

Emily Elizabeth gazed at Jetta. "I don't take things that don't belong to me."

Jetta wasn't really listening. She was reaching for her mirror.

"Hey!" she cried, surprised. "It's gone." She glared at Emily Elizabeth. "Give my mirror back, Emily Elizabeth. Right now!"

Emily Elizabeth gasped. "I didn't take it!"

"Just give it back!"

"I don't have it, Jetta," Emily Elizabeth said again. "I'm going home."

Mac's ears perked up. Something else was missing? He sat up, interested. This was something to report to Clifford!

🦴 Setting a Trap

Clifford was holding a detective meeting with Cleo and T-Bone.

"We have to prove Emily Elizabeth didn't take the medal," he said. "There's got to be a way."

Just then Mac raced over.

"Emily Elizabeth did it again!" he said excitedly. "This time she stole Jetta's mirror."

"Cut it out, Mac," Clifford said sharply.

"It had to be her," Mac told
him. "She was the only one there."

Cleo stepped closer to Clifford.
"Do you think she could have,
Clifford? Maybe she couldn't help
it. . . ."

Clifford held up a giant paw to

stop Cleo from talking. "No. Emily Elizabeth didn't do anything wrong. But I'm going to find out who did!"

He gazed at Cleo and her shiny new bow. He knew just what to do.

A few minutes later, Clifford and his friends peeked out from behind Emily Elizabeth's house.

Cleo's bow lay on the ground, twinkling in the afternoon sun. Clifford had placed it there.

Whoever took the medal and the mirror would surely take this shiny object, too, he thought. It was bait.

"Do you really think someone will try to steal your bow?" T-Bone asked Cleo.

Cleo shrugged. "Sure. Humans love shiny stuff."

They heard footsteps. A seabird squawked.

"Look!" Cleo whispered. "It's Emily Elizabeth! She's going to take it!"

"No, she won't," Clifford whispered back.

Clifford held his breath as Emily

Elizabeth stopped. She picked up the bow. She turned it this way and that, examining it closely.

Then she walked straight over to Cleo. "You lost your bow," Emily Elizabeth said. "Let me put it back in your hair."

Cleo lowered her head as Emily Elizabeth put the bow in place. She felt silly for thinking Emily Elizabeth would steal it.

"There!" said Emily Elizabeth. "It looks great."

"See? She didn't take it, Cleo!" T-Bone said after Emily Elizabeth walked away.

Cleo shook her head so the bow flew off. "No. But I wish someone would!"

"Come on, guys," Clifford told his friends. "Let's put it back on the sidewalk. We'll see if anyone else takes it."

"Right," said Cleo. She turned around to get it.

It was gone!

Mystery Solved!

"Oh, my gosh!" said Cleo. "Emily Elizabeth must have changed her mind. She came back to steal the bow!"

"She didn't take anything!" Clifford insisted. Why didn't anyone else believe that, too?

Then the dogs heard Jetta's voice. She was talking to Emily Elizabeth in front of her house.

"Okay, Emily Elizabeth. I'm going to give you one more

chance. Give back my medal and my mirror."

"I didn't take them, Jetta!" Emily Elizabeth said.

Clifford straightened up to his full height. Emily Elizabeth was down the street. She couldn't have taken the bow. He felt more

determined than ever. "We've got to find that medal!"

T-Bone circled the spot where Cleo had tossed the bow. "Look! There's a feather here. Just like the one in the park."

Squawk!

"And that sound!" T-Bone continued. "I heard it at the ferry dock. And I heard it again when Cleo's bow was taken!"

"Good work, T-Bone," said Clifford. "Those are just the clues we need!"

Squawk!

Clifford peered around. Where was that sound coming from?

T-Bone pointed high up in the sky. "It's that bird! Clifford! That bird is making all the noise!"

The bird landed in a tree. Clifford padded closer. He peered through the leaves. High up on a branch was the seabird, perched in a nest. The bird jumped as Clifford's nose pushed through the leaves.

"Wow!" Clifford barked happily. Now he could see the whole nest. It was filled with all sorts of shiny things. And there, right on top, were the medal, the mirror, and Cleo's bow! "Emily Elizabeth has to see this!" said Clifford.

🦴 A Loyal Friend

Clifford lifted Emily Elizabeth up to the seabird's nest.

"Oh!" Emily Elizabeth peered inside. "Clifford! It's Jetta's medal! You found it!"

"What are you doing?" Jetta called from the ground.

"Woof!" Mac barked beside her.

Gently, Clifford lowered Emily Elizabeth to the ground.

"Clifford found your medal,

Jetta!" Emily Elizabeth opened her hand and showed it to Jetta.

"What?" said Jetta.

Squawk!

Smiling, Emily Elizabeth pointed to the bird. "That old seabird must have taken it, and

your mirror, too. Some birds really like shiny things!"

Jetta took the medal, holding it close. "This is amazing!"

"I told you I didn't take it, Jetta," said Emily Elizabeth. "I wish you had believed me."

Jetta slumped, feeling bad. "I'm sorry. It just seemed like you did. But it wasn't fair for me to think that when I didn't know for sure."

Mac slinked close to the ground. He felt as bad as Jetta. "Wooof!" he whined, telling Clifford he was sorry.

Cleo nodded. She was sorry, too.

Clifford knelt close to Emily Elizabeth. He never thought she took anything. Not for an instant. Emily Elizabeth was his friend. And he believed in his friends.

Emily Elizabeth threw her arms around Clifford. "You never doubted me. Did you, Clifford?"

"Woof!"

"The most loyal friend I could ever have." Emily Elizabeth grinned at her Big Red Dog. "Clifford!"

MAKE ROOM

in your heart.

Now there's even more of him to love!
Watch *Clifford's Puppy Days*™ on PBS KIDS®!

scholastic.com/clifford

pbskids.org